To Lil, Sky, and Son for putting up with my occasional grumpy feet,
and to everyone who woke up with grumpy feet this morning,
I hope you find your baby unicorn.
L. S.

SIMON & SCHUSTER BOOKS FOR YOUNG READERS
An imprint of Simon & Schuster Children's Publishing Division
1230 Avenue of the Americas, New York, New York 10020
Copyright © 2016 by Lisa Stubbs
Originally published in 2016 in Great Britain by Boxer Books Limited
Published by arrangement with Boxer Books Limited
First US Edition 2017
All rights reserved, including the right of reproduction in whole or in part in any form.
SIMON & SCHUSTER BOOKS FOR YOUNG READERS is a trademark of Simon & Schuster, Inc.
For information about special discounts for bulk purchases, please contact Simon & Schuster
Special Sales at 1-866-506-1949 or business@simonandschuster.com.
The Simon & Schuster Speakers Bureau can bring authors to your live event. For more information or to book an event,
contact the Simon & Schuster Speakers Bureau at 1-866-248-3049 or visit our website at www.simonspeakers.com.
Book design by Tom Daly
The text for this book was set in Goudy Old Style.
The illustrations for this book were screen printed by the author.
Manufactured in China
0516 BOX
2 4 6 8 10 9 7 5 3 1
CIP data for this book is available from the Library of Congress.
ISBN 978-1-4814-7167-1
ISBN 978-1-4814-7168-8 (eBook)

Lily and Bear
Grumpy Feet

Lisa Stubbs

A Paula Wiseman Book
Simon & Schuster Books for Young Readers
New York London Toronto Sydney New Delhi

Lily loved to draw,
but today something
felt different.

Things felt a little frumpy
and bumpy, just not so and
not quite right.

The day was
too rainy,

the teapot was
too dribbly,
and the sunshine
color was missing.

Lily's pencils were too pointy,

her paint too sloshy,

and her crayons too stubby.

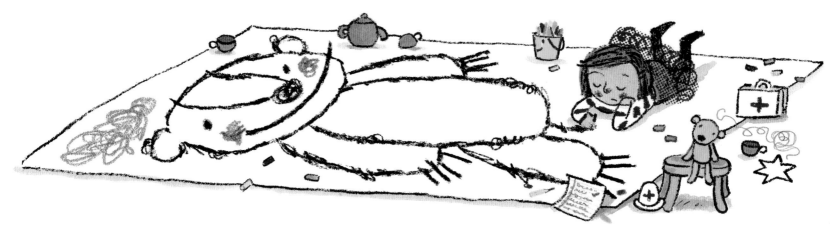

Everything felt grouchy and mouchy,
out of sorts and discombobbled.
Until Lily drew . . .

Things to do...
1. Draw bear ✓
2. Drive to the moon
3. ~~find~~ drink hot chocolate
4. polish stars
5. Jump really very high
6. find a baby unicorn

Bear!

So Bear put on his doctor's hat and stethoscope and listened.

It was clear to Bear what was wrong . . .

Lily had

grumpy feet!

Bear thought it would help
if Lily wore happy shoes.

But things still felt frumpy and bumpy, just not so and not quite right.

Lily's feet were still grumpy.

Bear thought
it might help
if Lily had some
sticky cake.

But Lily's feet were
still grumpy.

Lily took her grumpy feet
to sit in the toy box.

Bear looked at Lily's list and
had a marvelous idea.

He set to work immediately.

Bear squeezed into the
toy box next to Lily
and started the engine.
"Where are we going?"
asked Lily.

Bear drove past the rainy day, dribbly teapot, and missing sunshine color.

Past the pointy pencils, sloshy paint, and stubby crayons.

Past the happy shoes and the sticky fishy cake.

"To a place that glows all comfy, not frumpy and bumpy. It is very so and just right," said Bear, as they drove into the starry night.

They drank hot
chocolate and
polished the stars.
Then Bear played a
happy moon tune
on his banjo.

Lily's feet started
to tap and smile . . .

Lily's feet started
to wiggle and giggle . . .

really very high!

Lily's feet started
to laugh and jump . . .

Bear had turned the grumps
into the jumps!
There was only one thing left to do:

number 6 on Lily's list.

Find a baby unicorn . . .

and they did.